The BEAN Family Reunion

A REAL UNTRUE STORY

Written by Anna M. Ridley Etuk

ISBN-13: 978-1-7332561-1-7

Ridley-Etuk
Houston, TX

Cover and Interior Design by Tami Boyce (tamiboyce.com)

Dedication

I dedicate this piece of literature to my sons: Godwin and Andrew, my granddaughter, Kynnady, my beloved parents and family, former co-workers, former teachers, former students, and friends with respect and love.

Acknowledgment

I extend to my dear sister, Delilah R. Session, my sincerest gratitude for graciously and willingly accepting my request to critically read my manuscript and offer constructive criticism and suggestions for improvement. Thank you so much for being my second pair of eyes and perusing with different lenses.

No Beans, Please!

No beans? Inasmuch as beans are a global staple, and today are eaten by a huge percentage of people worldwide, you might be surprised to know that there was a time when humans stopped eating beans! As delicious and as diverse as they are, why did humans stop eating them for a period of time during the 19th century until the early twenty-first century?

To answer that question as succinctly as possible, there were several reasons that went viral and generated a lethal fear of being a bean eater.

First, since some beans have "eyes" people started thinking that the black eyes, yellow eyes, and the eye of the goat were staring at them from their bowls or plates. Even though the beans had been cooked, the "eyes" were still alive and continuously looking as if they dared anyone to spoon them up to his/her mouth. The "eyes" had an intimidating look that caused humans to pass on the beans. The "eyes" had it and they helped insure that beans would be exempt from the list of endangered species.

Jumping beans was another reason people discontinued beans in their diet. When attempts were made to prepare these beans for cooking, they started jumping everywhere! They could not be contained in one place. How could people eat beans that jumped out of their pots?

Then there were magic beans. The scare of magic beans as rumor proclaimed was that they would cast a spell on those who touched them, especially the black beans. Most people were aware of black magic and how horrific it could be.

Additionally, there was the notion that beans were poisonous. Many beans have lectins, toxins, which if ingested, had the potential to kill people. Who would want to die because of eating beans?

Beans were also put on the back burner because they filled humans up with toxic gas making them unpleasant to be in the company of others and causing bloating followed by a lot of anal blowouts.

Finally, humans suspended eating beans because of the evolution of the beans. Beans had eyes, could jump, cast spells, poison humans, and fuel them with gas. Beans took on personalities and started thinking and behaving like people. It became extremely difficult to eat beans that had become personified, Human Beans.

CHAPTER ONE

The Bean–Pea Family

The Bean-Pea family is phenomenally HUGE having members from all over the world.

Many who have studied the origin of the Bean-Pea family debate its genealogy and history. Where did this one come from, and where did that one come from? Some documents show the origin of all beans is in Meso-America/Andes.

This book narrates the story of the Bean-Pea family as fictitiously as possible as it developed in the United States from the 19th century until the 21st century.

In the beginning, traders, immigrants, and travelers from various parts of the world brought the beans and peas with them when they came to the United States of America (USA). However, some beans and peas found their own way and met other Beans or Peas and started their families. For example, one of the oldest Beans, Garbanzo, from Mexico met Pea. They fell in love, married, and migrated to the USA as Mr. Garbanzo Bean and Mrs. Pea Bean. A few years after they settled into their new farm home, they decided it was time to reproduce themselves.

Bean babies are not born alive like human babies. Bean and Pea babies have to be planted in soil, watered, and exposed to sunlight. Another thing that's different about Beans and Peas is that both father and mother can produce more of their kind. So Garbanzo could bear more Garbanzos and Pea could reproduce more Peas.

One night when there was a full, silvery moon indicating the time was right for bean planting, Garbanzo and Pea dug holes for themselves, jumped in, covered up, and waited for the Spring showers.

After a few days, the rain came. It rained violently for several days giving the Beans and other plants a

generous drink. Both Garbanzo and Pea began sprouting. They grew side by side into beautiful distinguished plants.

They had been growing for one week when the owner of the farm came by. He was amazed to find two plants that he had not planted. Though he could not figure out how they got there, he appreciated them and took good care of them. He put poles in the ground and tied Pea up so that she could grow spiraling around them. Garbanzo, being a bush bean, did not need any poles. No more than two weeks passed when Pea had an offspring – a new little Pea-Bean! They named her Wavy Bean.

Meanwhile, they waited for Garbanzo to grow a Bean. Finally, a little Garbanzo appeared and they named him Garbanzo Bean, Jr.

CHAPTER TWO

Branching Out

By this time, Wavy had grown into a sizable and adorable Pea. Her mother, Pea, had so many more children. Since Wavy was the oldest, she decided to detach herself from Pea and go find her own life's path. She grew to be such a sweetheart that everywhere she went, people loved her dearly especially the Navy seals. They loved her so much and she became so popular, they started calling her Navy Bean, though she was a pea.

Garbanzo, Jr. saw what Wavy did. He liked the idea and decided to follow in her footsteps. His story ended very differently but great nonetheless.

When he detached from Garbanzo, Sr. who also had many other Beans, a bird pecked him up and took him away to a new place with intent to eat him later. As the bird flew higher and higher, Garbanzo, Jr. wiggled and wiggled until he freed himself from the grip of the bird's beak. He fell from such a height that when he hit the ground, he was buried alive! He could not uncover himself. In fact, the more he tried to free himself, the deeper he found himself. At the point of total exhaustion, his struggle for freedom ended. He realized that he was not going to overcome his captive state, so he surrendered, relaxed, and waited for whatever would result.

Needless to say, he sprouted, grew, and bore Garbanzo Beans. Oh how he grew Garbanzo Beans! As soon as the first batch of Beans was harvested, another one was ready. This went on throughout that bean season. Though humans did not eat the Beans, they fed them to their farm animals and used them for other purposes.

All of Garbanzo's Beans stayed attached to him until they were harvested. When the season ended, two Beans were left on the ground near Garbanzo, Jr. He thought that they should be distinguishable, so he named them

Fred Bean and Ted Bean. Unfortunately, a few days later, a hurricane came and flooded the land near and far. The water took Fred one way and Ted another.

Garbanzo, Jr. was grief stricken with the thought of never knowing where Fred and Ted had been taken as well as not being able to get up and go searching for them. So like his mother and father, he remained in place and continued to bear more Beans season after season.

Fred and Ted started their independent lives in their new places.

Fred was very outgoing and jovial. Socializing was his cup of tea. One day, he met the love of his life, Red. It truly was love at first sight. Feeling that he could not allow her to slip away from him, he quickly proposed marriage to her. She accepted. Shortly after, they married becoming Mr. Fred Bean and Mrs. Red Bean. They became a very popular couple in their area. Red Bean, however, was much more popular than Fred.

They, like their parents, decided to help increase the Bean family's population, so they went through the process that Beans must go through to have more Beans. Fred had Garbanzos and Red had Red Beans. Year after year, both had prolific Bean bearing seasons. Some of their off-springs were harvested, or eaten by birds and other animals. Some were blown away and some were swept away by rain and flood water. Fred and Red remained in place and continued reproducing season after season.

Unlike Fred, Ted was an introvert. He had no friends or acquaintances. He became depressed at being separated from his familiar environment and his family especially his brother, Fred.

Day after day and month after month his melancholy state grew and grew to the thickness of the mud in the Mississippi River.

Two years passed. Then one bright, sunny day, Ted discovered something that he had longed for, another Bean! They introduced themselves and with the passage of time, they developed a friendship which helped Ted overcome his state of deep depression. They shared their life stories and discovered that they were cousins. They began to confide in each other.

One day as they were talking, Cousin Pinto told Cousin Ted that he wanted a wife and family. Ted confessed that he did, too.

As destiny would have it, both met and married beautiful twin sisters Lima and Butter. Ted married Lima and Pinto married Butter. Now there were two lovely couples, Mr. Ted Bean and Mrs. Lima Bean and Mr. Pinto Bean and Mrs. Butter Bean.

They searched for a place to call home and finally found their ideal spots. Not long after settling in, they decided to start their families. They became historical and did what Beans do to have children. They repeated the reproduction process. Each one dug a hole, jumped in, covered up, and waited for rain and sunshine. It didn't take too long before Ted bore Garbanzos and Lima had large and baby Lima Beans. Pinto had Pinto Beans and Butter had Butter Beans. Some of the Beans were harvested and some were taken away to new territories in various ways, but Ted and Lima and Pinto and Butter remained in place and continued to reproduce.

One of Ted's sons and two of his daughters who were taken away rose to fame. His son, Pickett Bean or Dean P. Bean, became a well- known leader in his community. The two daughters married and were recognized as having more Beans than any of the other Beans in the whole Bean family.

The Beans did not always know their relatives because of the way they were separated when they were too young to remember.

One day out of somewhere a stately, tall, male Bean found his way to a meeting of the Beans. He introduced himself to all of the Beans as Black Bean. He was very suave with smooth, ebony black, flawless skin. He had the eyes of all the single ladies. Because of a physical attraction, each fantasized about becoming his bride. There was a problem with those thoughts. He was a relative!

However, when the time came, Black Bean chose a wife. Though she was a Bean, she and Black were not related. What a co-incident! Her name was White. They became Mr. Black Bean and Mrs. White Bean.

After a few months, like all the other Beans, they did what Beans do to have little Beans. He had Black Beans and she had White Beans. Some of their little ones were harvested and some were taken away by various means. Black and White Bean remained in place and continued having more Black and White Beans.

After several generations of Beans had been established, the Bean family's traditions began to disappear. For instance, instead of settling down and remaining in one place after marrying or not marrying, the youngest Beans discovered that they could travel and go places by land, air, and sea. They could have a much more enriched and interesting life than their previous generations. Their lives could be filled with fun and excitement made possible with a multitude of technological devices and machines.

Beans hopped on planes, ships, buses, trains, motorcycles or whatever could transport them from place to place including their own personal cars. Beans sprang up everywhere. Because they did not know their roots, when one Bean met another, they did not know how or if they were related.

CHAPTER THREE

Meeting of Pink Bean and The Great Northern Bean (The GNB)

Pink Bean is a Bean who loves to travel. Just say, "Go," and she is ready. However, it had been a while since she had taken a trip, so she decided to get away for a few days and enjoy the freedom and relaxation that a vacation can bring. She planned a quiet, uneventful trip.

The following week, she packed her bags and went back to her home town in Mexico where she had made hotel reservations for five days. Her flight took four hours. Since she was bursting with energy upon arrival, she did not stay in her hotel room. She went about revisiting places of interest and exploring new places. She discovered that some places that were there the last time she was there had either been replaced or were non-existent. Nonetheless, she fully enjoyed her day of exploration.

She thought her arrival in Mexico would go unnoticed and be of no interest to anyone. But to her amazement, another Bean, The Great Northern Bean (The GNB) had been informed that she had come to town. He was one who, through his informants, knew everything that went on in the town no matter how insignificant or phenomenal it might be. So while Pink was there, The GNB wanted to meet her to find out if they are kinfolks.

On the second day after her arrival, The GNB sent his messenger to meet Pink and arrange a meeting for them. At first, Pink was very reluctant and skeptical about agreeing to meet The GNB at his house. But the more the messenger told her about how influential and renowned The GNB had become in the town and surrounding areas, the less hesitant she became about meeting him.

Finally, she consented to meeting him at his home at 10:00 AM on Thursday. The messenger was thrilled that he had accomplished his goal, so he departed with good news to relay to The GNB.

Hearing that Pink had acquiesced to the meeting, The GNB became overwhelmed with joy and excitement for he rarely got the opportunity to meet other Beans.

Thursday rolled around and Pink prepared herself for the grand meeting with The GNB. He sent his messenger to pick her up and deliver her to his residence where he was waiting with great expectancy and anticipation that Pink would be a relative.

The messenger picked Pink up and drove for about 15 minutes before arriving and parking at the home of The GNB. Pink was quite impressed with the exterior appearance of the home. It was very awe-inspiring. One might think that a person of nobility lived there.

When the messenger opened the car door for Pink, she got out and he escorted her into the house where The

GNB awaited her arrival. They exchanged greetings and The GNB invited her to sit, relax, and enjoy some refreshing cool water, and other items he had prepared. Pink accepted.

Her perspective of the interior of the home was similar to that of the exterior. She asked The GNB if he were married since there had been no mention of a Mrs. GNB.

The GNB began to narrate his story. He told Pink that he had been married for 35 years before his wife, Greta, became ill and finally died of complications from an incurable bean fever. Pink expressed her condolences. The GNB thanked her for her sentiments. As they continued, The GNB informed Pink that he has been a widower for 20 years. Then he asked Pink about her marital status. She responded that she was single and had never been married and never had any offsprings.

As their dialogue progressed, The GNB shared with Pink that he and Greta had many, many offsprings. Several lived in different parts of the world. He showed her some pictures of his family and explained who was who, what they were doing, and

where they were. Pink was delighted to see how fruitful The GNB's life had been.

At this juncture, the conversation changed its focus. Each had noticed that they had some characteristics in common, so they began to talk about themselves to help determine whether or not they were related. It wasn't long before they concluded that they were relatives.

Since they had had an extensive and diverse conversation, Pink was growing weary, so she suggested that they exchange contact information in order to keep in touch. She decided to say good-bye and return to the hotel. The messenger was summoned and he returned Pink to her hotel where she had a peaceful night as she reflected on the day's experience with The GNB.

A day after meeting the Great Northern Bean, Pink returned to the USA. When she got back, she thought about her meeting with him and decided to host a Bean Family get together.

First, she called the Great Northern Bean and discussed it with him. He liked the idea and agreed to call and invite all of the Beans in Mexico. She planned everything: venue, who, and when. She made sure every detail had been thoroughly thought out and was easily executable. After concluding her plans, Pink called The GNB again and gave him all the necessary information and suggested that he move forward with inviting the Beans in Mexico.

CHAPTER FOUR

Union of the Beans

After receiving the invitation from The Great Northern Bean, some of the other Beans in Mexico decided to call the Beans they knew in Central and South America and invite them. They not only called but sent verbal messages and mailed invitations as well.

Pink invited Beans in the U. S. who knew Beans in other parts of the world. They all were invited.

All the Beans were getting more and more excited about having a Bean family get together (Union). Some would be coming to the U. S. and meeting other Beans for the first time except Pink and The Great Northern Bean who had met earlier in Mexico.

Pink and The GNB kept planning and putting everything in place for that great day when they would all get together for fun, food, fellowship, and family.

Pink had started a count down until the day of the gathering. The day finally arrived. On that day, Beans arrived in a constant stream one after the other and family after family. Before long, Pink's house was spilling over with Beans of many sizes, shapes, and colors. A few Peas came, too, claiming that they were rightly part of the Bean family because their great grandma was Pea Bean who had married Garbanzo Bean nicknamed "Chickpea."

When they thought that all of the Beans had arrived, they started the party. Pink introduced herself and welcomed them. Next, she told them that she wanted to get to know her relatives and where they live. She loves traveling and if she visits a place, she would like to spend time with her relatives who live there.

After Pink finished, The GNB spoke and told them about himself. Then he conducted a roll call to register every Bean and Pea present. Each Bean had a distinguished color, marking, shape, or size to help with identification.

Black Beans, White Beans, Red Beans, Pinto Beans, Green Beans, Wax Beans, String Beans, Snap Beans, Navy Beans, Lima Beans, Butter Beans, Cannellini Beans, Mung Beans, Pea Beans, Soy Beans, Harricot Beans, Cranberry Beans, Garbanzo Beans, Anasazi Beans, Adzuki Beans, Coffee Beans, Vanilla Beans, Cocoa Beans, and the sweetest of all the Beans, Jelly Beans. Let us not forget Kidney Beans. It wasn't a hill of beans but a mountain of Beans.

They had a great time getting to meet and greet each other and seeing how big the Bean family is.

The party lasted for over three hours. As it was winding down, the doorbell rang. Who could that be? Pink opened the door to find a pair of twin Beans: Fava Bean and Broad Bean. Their flight had been delayed twice. They were fortunate enough to arrive before anyone left. With new Beans in the house, no one could leave just yet. More fun, food, and family.

Laisse les bons temps rouler was the atmosphere at the party. Abruptly the music inside the house stopped because there was music outside the house as though there was a parade. They heard horns, drums, cymbals, and whistles. What in the world was going on? The music grew louder and louder as the band neared Pink's house. Was it indeed a parade? No. It wasn't a holiday. It wasn't a high school marching band practicing. Who or what was it? The Soldier Beans had decided to surprise the family with a grand military arrival of pomp, flare, and swing.

They marched to Pink's house calling out and echoing, "Give me a B-B. Give me an E-E. give me an A-A. give me an N-N. B-E-A-N family. B-E-A-N family.

The Bean family as well as all the neighbors were excited and impressed that the Soldier Beans had performed so well publicly while displaying their love and loyalty to their family- the Beans.

With the arrival of the Soldier Beans, there was not enough room inside Pink's house, so they had to start a lawn party with live entertainment. The Soldier Beans played lively dancing music and everyone was in the groove until something happened to Snappie. Oh my gosh, did Snappie snap! After all, she was a snap Bean. She turned the party out with all attention drawn to herself. She became excessively loud, emotional, and restless. Everyone tried to calm her down, but to no avail. She snapped multi-directional, north, south, east, and west and everywhere in between. She screamed, stomped, ran in circles, and shouted, "No! No!"" she was highly enraged. There was no visible evidence leading to why Snappie lost her cool. Everybody was looking around and at each other with questioning countenances. What happened? The only reply was, "I don't know." Snappie kept on snapping for almost fifteen minutes! By this time, the party mood had fizzled. Everyone was ready to go. When Snappie realized that she was the party pooper, she calmed herself down and apologized to the family. The GNB asked her why she snapped, and she said the Soldier Beans played a song that brought back bad memories from her adolescent years. Though everyone accepted her apology, the party was over with no chance of resurrection. No bouncing back.

Pink Bean and The GNB thanked everyone for coming and announced that they were going to begin planning another family gathering, a reunion, in the next

two years and that it will be bigger and better than this one- the Union of the Beans.

Split Pea was the first to split the scene. Then everyone else followed her lead. Within a very short time, the whole city of Beanville was overflowing with Beans. They were in buses, taxis, subway trains, at the airport, and of course on the freeways in their personal cars. The Soldier Beans were on foot marching back to the park and ride where they had met and started their march to Pink's house.

Citizens of the town were amazed and overwhelmed to see such an assortment of Beans together at one time. They could not resist gazing at them and some small children even pointed some out i.e. Black Beans, Red Beans, Pinto Beans, Navy Beans, … Some of the children even tried to count the Beans.

Meanwhile, while waiting for her flight at the airport, Snappie could not restrain herself from being a snap Bean. She pin-pointed a child pointing at her. This she could not tolerate. She became enraged and lost it again. She snapped at the child, "Why are you pointing at me? Haven't you seen a snap Bean before? Stop pointing at me!" She was so loud and her voice was piercing. It made the boy run to his parents. Snappie followed him to the next row over from where she was waiting. She snapped at the boy's parents, too. "You need to teach your child some manners. It's impolite to point at Beans.!" The parents apologized and suggested that Snappie should calm down. Snappie snapped, "I am a real snap Bean and I snap when I want to. I'm supposed to snap. I would not be a snap Bean if I did not snap!"

Having finished her snapping, Snappie emotionlessly returned to her place and quietly waited to board her plane.

After that incident, the other passengers who witnessed it, did not even dare to look at Snappie let alone say anything to her.

Boarding for Snappie's flight was finally announced. She and all the other travelers entered the plane peacefully. However, Snappie misread the seat number on her ticket and sat in the wrong seat. Shortly after getting her carry-on in the overhead compartment and sitting down, the passenger assigned to that seat arrived. It was another snap Bean, Slap Bean. Snappie and Slap had it out about the seat. They argued back and forth. "This is my seat. It's not your seat. It's mine!" Clearly their argument was a major disturbance on the plane. Slap Bean had a shorter fuse than Snappie. Just as Slap was getting ready to slap Snappie, two plane security officers appeared and intervened. One of the officers asked to see their tickets. When he looked at them, he pointed out to Snappie that she was in Slap's seat.

Embarrassed, Snappie took her belongings, vacated the seat and followed quietly as the officer escorted her to the right seat. She felt disgraced and subdued but acknowledged that she was out of order. She peacefully sat in the right place. In a covert way, all eyes were on her but no one wanted her to spot them looking at her for fear of sending her into another snapping rage. They had had enough of her snaps.

Snappie, too, was tired of snapping, so she settled herself, put on her headphones and patiently waited for the plane to take off. Everyone kept their fingers crossed that there would be no more encounters with Snappie.

Finally, the plane had a smooth lift off and Snappie fell asleep. No one, not even the flight attendants disturbed her in any way. She slept throughout the flight without dinner, snack, or anything to drink.

Eight hours later, the plane reached Karibean Island and landed successfully. Snappie, Slap, and all the other Beans deboarded, collected their luggage, and said, "Good-bye." It was Snappie who called out, "See you at the reunion." Since everyone on the plane was a snap Bean, they understood what she meant.

Slap Bean, became excited and led the Beans in a parade out of the airport using the chant that the Soldier Beans had marched to. Courageously and thunderously she called "Give me a B-B. Give me an E -E. Give me an A-A. Give me an N-N. B-E-A-N family. B-E-A-N family. They kept this up until the chant dissipated and completely faded away as they all headed home anticipating the next family bash. Being back on the island seemed to make Snappy happy.

CHAPTER FIVE

Preparation

All the Beans had been back home for about a year now and they were still talking about and reflecting on the fun of the union and looking forward to the adventures of the reunion.

To rev up more excitement for the upcoming event, Snappie and Slap got together and posted pictures and videos of the Bean Family Union on their social media pages. They thought that doing so would draw attention to and build interest in what was in store for the Beans' future.

Meanwhile, Pink and The GNB were busy trying to secure a place big enough to hold all the Beans who had attended the Union plus all the ones who would be first timers. They investigated banquet halls, hotel ballrooms, party halls, and community centers, but none were large enough since new Beans had started sprouting up from everywhere; Beans that neither Pink nor The GNB had ever heard of.

After carefully weighing the pros and cons of each venue, they agreed to hold it outdoors as they had ended up doing at the union. The Beach of Beanville or the water park became the last two options for the reunion.

Though the beach had pavilions, picnic areas, restrooms, and water, it did not have as many amenities as the water park and neither was it as large. So because of size, entertainment, and hotel accommodations, Pink and The GNB decided to reserve the water park for two and a half days for the first Bean Family Reunion.

They were glad to have accomplished the task of location for the biggest event ever in the history of the Bean family. Now all the phone calls, location visitations, price comparisons, inquiries regarding availability, and making reservations was behind them, they could move forward with other preparations.

Pink and The GNB knew that just the two of them could not handle every aspect of the reunion, therefore, they compiled a list of committees and who they would ask to lead them.

One thing they had learned from the union was NOT to put Snappie in charge of any committee because she is too quick to snap. They did not make any snap decisions but took their time in carefully making selections based on personality traits that they had observed being displayed at the Union.

The committees included:
Publicity
Entertainment/Games
Food
Accommodations
Financial
Clean Up
Security
Program
Reunion Shirt

With committee list in hand, Pink and The GNB revisited the registry from the union. They had a very lengthy discussion about who should be assigned to each committee. Finally, after several hours, they concluded the following:

Committee	Responsible Party
Publicity	Red Beans
Entertainment	Jelly Beans
Food	Green Beans
Accommodations	Coffee Beans
Financial Affairs	Black Beans
Reunion Shirt	White Beans
Clean Up	Vanilla Beans
Security	Soldier/Navy Beans
Program	Garbanzo Beans

Having finalized the list of responsible parties, the next task was to inform each group of its role and duties. Tirelessly working to get it together, Pink and The GNB sent out a letter to one member of each group requesting them to accept the assigned responsibility. The last part of the letter asked them to reply indicating whether or not they would be able to honor the request.

The GNB and Pink waited patiently for the replies. After a few weeks, the replies started coming in. The Soldier Beans were the first responders with an affirmative reply. Next, the Green Beans said, "Yes." Then the Red Beans, Black Beans, and Jelly Beans' responses came on the same day. All replied, "Yes, we will." Responses continued to stream in until the final one from the Vanilla Beans arrived. It, too, like all the others said, "Yes. Of course we will."

As each reply came in, Pink informed The GNB. They were so excited about all the positive responses. With that task completed, Pink and The GNB could relax a little knowing that the family of Beans would be in charge of everything pertaining to the reunion. Aa-ah!

A couple of months passed and reunion time was drawing nearer. Pink and The GNB started contacting the delegates to see how far they had gone with their assignment. All of them had been enthusiastically working to take care of their responsibilities.

After talking with each committee leader, Pink and The GNB decided that it was time to send out a family newsletter to officially inform everyone about the details related to the reunion. So they got together and composed a letter that read:

WANTED!

Who? Beans

What? 1st Annual Bean Family Reunion

Where? Beanville Water Park- 1784 Beanstalk Blvd. – District of Beanville U. S. A.-70999

When? Bean Fest Weekend – September 2 – 4

Register online at www.nothingbutbeans.org. Reunion fee of $25.00/pp due with registration. Beanie babies and bambeanos ages 0 – 3 years and seniors 80+ free. Purchase your reunion shirt at www.whitebean.org. Hotel information and reservations at www.coffeebean.org.

Join us for an exciting weekend of family, food, fellowship, and fun. More of everything you experienced at the union starting at 7:00 AM daily. Don't miss it! See you there.

When it was ready, Pink and The GNB used the registry of the union to send the letter out to the members of the Bean family.

The Red Beans publicized the event in the local newspapers, on radio, and via social media networks.

Everything was falling into place well and the green light was definitely on and glowing brightly for the event. Time began passing swiftly as the big day approached.

With one month, nine days, and nine hours to go, Pink and The GNB's phones were hotlines ringing off the hook. Calls kept coming throughout the day and mid- way through the night. Either someone had a question or a committee had an update to share. Relief from all this phone madness would come once the reunion had come and gone.

CHAPTER SIX

The Day Before the Reunion

SEPTEMBER 1

Beanville was flooded with members of the Bean family. News of the reunion had reached far and wide. The town had to accommodate the humans coming for the Bean Fest as well as the Beans attending their reunion.

As it turned out, there was space for everybody with room to spare. Most of the Bean family had booked reservations at the Beanville Luxury Inn & Suites, the city's largest and most upscale hotel having a 5- star rating. They had gotten a great rate because the reservation committee had negotiated the price.

The Beans who did not get in at the Beanville Luxury Inn & Suites were housed in neighboring hotels throughout the city. There wasn't a hotel around that did not have some Beans booked.

With visitors for the Bean Fest and a multitude of Beans in the city, imagine how crowded the local businesses, especially the restaurants were! The movie theaters, malls, strip shops, museums, other attractions and places of interest looked like they were having a Black Friday sale.

Public transportation vehicles were as busy as bees with constant streams of Beans, tourists, and Beanville residents coming and going-a conglomerate of organized chaos. There were a lot of smart Beans finding their way around the town and through the shopping malls. However, having so many personalities around, there must have been at least one bean head in the mix who didn't know beans about what was going on.

It was now mid-day and the countdown to the opening day of the reunion was rapidly approaching. Some of the Beans wanted to attend the Bean Fest while others wanted to go shopping. Yet others wanted to just relax at the pool side or in their hotel rooms.

The clock kept ticking. Day faded into evening, and evening into night. There were still things to do before you know what. Eat dinner, watch a movie, sightsee, admire the night lights, play some games, and finally get some sleep. Wake up the next morning and voila! The first day of the 1st Annual Bean Family Reunion.

CHAPTER 7

The Reunion

SEPTEMBER 2 – DAY 1
MEET THE FAMILY

No more waiting or anticipating. It was family reunion time! From the beanie babies and bambeanos to Snappie, everybody was happy and feeling proud to be a part of the Bean family. The Beanville Hotel had their family name boldly illuminated on its marquee: Bean Family – Welcome to Beanville.

The daily itineraries had been posted on the Bean Family webpage so they all knew the what, when, and where scheduled for each day.

The first activity of each day was breakfast at the breakfast bar in the water park from 7:00 AM – 10:00 AM. Games, entertainment, and other activities were planned between breakfast and lunch as well as between lunch and dinner.

The Green Beans, Jelly Beans, and Garbanzo Beans got to the water park two hours ahead of everyone else, 5:00 AM because they had to make sure that things were all setup and in place by 7:00 when the family would start coming with readiness to satisfy their healthy appetites.

Everything was set just right in expectation of the family's arrival. Even the weather was no threat to the day's activities. No news of tropical depressions, hurricanes, or any type of storm or inclement weather. The forecast indicated sunshiny days with temperatures ranging between 70 – 85 degrees F for the next seven days. The weather condition was perfect for a perfect outdoor reunion.

The Green Beans looked at the clock which showed 7:00 AM. They looked at the Jelly Beans and the Garbanzo Beans who looked back at them. They all looked toward the entrance to see the first enthusiastic arrivals. Everyone from the union and tons of unmet relatives were all lined up waiting for instructions on how to proceed through breakfast.

From the responses that they had received, the committee expected a large turnout so they were prepared with more than ample feeding and watering stations.

After everyone had found a place and taken a seat, the chairbean of the Jelly Beans opened breakfast with greetings, welcome, and blessing of the food. When she said, "Let the eating begin," a thunderous roar of voices and applause went up to the sky and easy listening music began playing in the background.

Since Beans eat with their roots, they could not get up and socialize while having their roots embedded in soil or water. By the way, the preferred drink of Beans is not coffee, tea, hot chocolate, or sodas like humans, but simple plain, atmospheric temperature water. It's what they go for every time, morning, noon, or night and any drink in between.

Breakfast was going as planned. Everyone was having a fantastic time. Seeing the array of Beans gathered together in one place at the same time was a treat by itself.

Time for introductions was fast approaching as breakfast was coming to an end. Pink made an announcement informing her family that breakfast was wrapping up and that The GNB would facilitate the next activity: Introductions.

Everybody was quite anxious for the introductions because there were so many colors, patterns, shapes, and sizes.

Those who were at the union had met previously, but there were so many newcomers that the situation demanded introductions.

Now that breakfast was over, The GNB introduced himself and Pink Bean. He also briefly outlined the roots of the reunion.

When he finished his speech, he did a roll call starting with the members who had attended the union. Knowing her behavior type, their eyes began searching for Snappie. When she sensed that she was the center of attention, she came front and center and very calmly and cordially introduced herself and identified with vine Beans. She did not create any drama. In fact, she seemed to be very jovial and content. She left them wondering for how long would it be before an eruption.

After Snappie, each one who went to the union introduced himself/herself and his/her family until the last one. They were all there. The GNB called for a round of applause for them. They had come to both events, the union and the reunion.

First time attendees were called. What an outstanding time this was. There were national as well as international Beans present, too many to account for on these pages. However, to mention a few: Dutch Bullet Bean; Dragon Tongue Bean; Eye of the Goat (Ojo de Cabra); Calypso Bean; Good Mother Stallard, Ireland Creek Annie, Kentucky Wonder, Preacher Bean; Yellow Eye Bean; Molasses Face Bean; Rattlesnake Bean; Purple King and Queen Bean; Mayacoba Bean from Peru; Ewa Oloyin (Honey Bean) all the way from Nigerian in West Africa; Red Swan Bean; Tiger's Eye Bean; Turkey Craw Bean; Zolfino Bean; and Tongue of Fire Bean. Continuing there were Flageolet Bean from France; Cannellini Bean from Argentina and some from Italy also there were the Manchurian Beans from N. E. Asia/China. Here a Bean. There a Bean. Everywhere a Bean! Wow!

It seemed as though introductions would last to infinity, but that activity did finally end. No one became bored because of the interesting names, similarities, and differences. Best of all, they were all part of the Bean family.

After the introductions, they took a 60-minute break giving time for mingling and refreshing.

They were amazed at the make-up of the Bean family especially knowing that somewhere in the world, there were still more Beans.

When the break ended, it was a favorite time – lunch.

Breakfast rules applied to lunch and later to dinner as well. Everyone who wanted to eat and drink, found a spot. As they began to partake, lively music started to play to encourage an atmosphere of celebration. Since not everyone ate lunch, there was time for talking, dancing, walking, and table games. Some strolled around the water park investigating future activities.

While so many things were going on, the Soldier and Navy Beans were on guard making sure that the area was secure and the safety of the Bean family was not compromised.

When lunchtime ended, the Jelly Beans called the family to order in order to prepare for a game as well as get to know each other better. Before they could play the game, they had to put themselves into two groups – bush Beans and vine Beans. That meant more mingling and talking to each other.

They all started interacting by asking for names, addresses, phone numbers and whether they were a vine or a bush Bean. This activity lasted for quite a while since the Beans are an extensive family.

After an hour and a half, Snappie became restless and cried out, "ELMO! ELMO!" she repeated. No one knew what she meant, so The GNB asked her what did she mean by "ELMO." She said, "Enough! Leave it. Move on." Her outcry resonated with others, and indeed, they moved on.

The lead Jelly Bean, Jell, announced that it was time to find out "Who's Who." First she called for the vine Beans to stand. Snappie, Slap, and String Bean immediately sprang up as if they were going up a beanstalk. Others stood, too. When the vine Beans were all standing, Jell asked them to form one group to her left.

The bush Beans who were seated, had to group themselves to the right. Among them were Jacob's Gold Bean, Provider Bean, Calypso, and a multitude of others.

There were as many vine Beans as there were bush Beans. With the two groups identified, they were all set to play a game scheduled for Day 2.

Day 1's agenda came to an end when Jell made an announcement pertaining to the remainder of the day. She told them that they had free time to explore and enjoy the water park and the city. Dinner would be from 6:00 PM – 9:00 PM and breakfast would commence at 7:00 AM. She thanked them for coming and participating in today's activities and aroused their interest in Day 2 by telling them that there would be competitions: vine Beans vs bush Beans.

Music began to play and the Beans began dispersing to their places of choice. With so many Beans around, you can imagine what kinds of things they got into before closing their eyes in anticipation of Day 2.

Soldier and Navy Beans kept watch throughout the night ensuring that the Beans' safety was not in jeopardy.

THE SILENT ARRIVAL OF THE
LOCUST BEANS

On the second day of the reunion, the Locust Beans swarmed into Beanville.

How Did They Find Their Way to the Reunion? It's a LONG story!

The Locust Beans had gotten the news about the Bean Family Reunion by word of mouth. Iru, a Locust Bean from Nigeria was visiting a renowned park in Kenya and happened to overhear some Kenyan Beans talking about and planning to attend the reunion in the United States.

When he heard that Beans from all over the world are going to be there, he imagined a United Nations of Beans.

After getting the necessary details relevant to the reunion, Iru thought about the possibility of the Locust Beans having a presence at the event. He became preoccupied with thoughts of how to make it happen since they are such a long distance away. He also thought about how other Locust Beans would respond to the idea.

He knew that:

The Bean family is planning a Reunion
It is scheduled for September 2 – 4 in the District of
Beanville, USA
Beans from every nation are invited.

Having this information, he decided that when he returned to Nigeria, he would present it to the other Locust Beans at their next family meeting which was coming up in two weeks.

Since he wanted to discuss this news about the Bean Family Reunion with his family he stayed in Kenya for only a few more days then flew back home using the power and energy of his own wings. Locust Beans are unique in that they can fly. Iru is a special Locust because he is multilingual. Since he is fluent in English, going to the USA will not present any communication barriers.

Upon his return home Iru planned his presentation and thought about possible objections to attending the event and how he would defend his position on their participation.

When it was time for the Locust's Family Meeting, Iru was ready. He had been on the internet at the library and found websites and social media pages related to the Bean Family Reunion, and he prepared to share his findings. He anticipated growing interest and excitement particularly among the young to middle aged Locusts.

Time for the meeting was at hand, so a swarm of Locusts gathered and flew to the "Meeting Tree." The meeting convened promptly at 6:00 PM. They were able to follow the agenda as written.

Iru's presentation fell under New Business, so he had to wait until near the end to do his presentation.

When at last he had the opportunity, he started by asking questions: "Did you know that our family, the Beans, had a union two years ago? How many Beans do you know who live in other parts of the world? Would you take advantage of the chance to get to meet other Beans?" Next he told them about the Bean Family Reunion taking place this year. He gave details about the reunion and encouraged attendance.

He promoted this as being a chance of a lifetime which may not be repeated. He gave them websites to checkout for more information. Since this was the first time any of his family, Locusts, had heard about the union and re-union, they were not ready to decide on what to do. They tabled the idea until the next meeting when they would have had more time to investigate, explore options, and weigh the pros and cons of taking such a long journey into an unchartered, distant land.

Between meetings, as they talked among themselves, some developed an optimistic perspective while others were pessimistic. However, from discussions that Iru was engaged in, seemingly there were more green lights than red.

Little by little, time for the next meeting came and Iru was extremely anxious to reach the verdict on whether or not they would be going.

Various ones elaborated on their position for and against going. The older ones were seriously concerned about health issues, fitness, and inconveniences of being away from the comfort of their homes and familiar environments. Also, they questioned safety. Could everyone get there safely and back?

The young ones who had never left the continent before were two thumbs up in favor of taking the trip. No matter what challenges presented themselves, they felt they could handle them.

After numerous opinions had been heard, it was time to vote- Yeah, we go or Nay, we stay at home.

Overwhelmingly, the vote yielded in favor, Yeah, we go. The youngsters gathered in swarm formation and flew in a circle around the "Meeting Tree", to celebrate the outcome of the vote. Iru was quite jubilant, too, so he joined the swarm. The beating of their wings together sounded like a thunderstorm.

After encircling the tree for the third time, they returned to their places with smiles on their faces expecting to plan the next steps. How to proceed would be on the agenda for the next meeting.

This evening's meeting progressed on to adjournment. When they dismissed, there was singing, dancing, shouting, clapping, jumping, and swarming. An incredible array of joyous emotions was on display demonstrating how elated most of them were because they were going somewhere away from home. Hip-hip hooray!

Iru, their self- appointed leader, was well pleased with the outcome of the vote and the expressions of excitement that had been exhibited after the meeting. He, now, knew that he had to be charismatic as well as diplomatic in his leadership role.

To keep the momentum going and strike the iron while it was hot, Iru called an emergency meeting at the "Meeting Tree" a week later.

As the days before the meeting passed, there was a lot of buzzing going on about going to the Bean Family Reunion. Almost all of the Locusts who planned to attend had ideas about the logistics of getting there.

In the meantime, Iru was planning the meeting's agenda. They would discuss topics such as: Who would be there? How will they travel? Safety; Lodging; Feeding/Hydration; Introductions; and participation in the reunion.

By and by, the meeting countdown ended and it was time to start. Iru called the meeting to order and began discussing the first item on the agenda: Who would be there? He told them that Beans from almost every nation, creed, size, shape, and color are going to be there. He went on to enumerate a few which he had found on the Bean family website. He mentioned Garbanzos and

Great Northern Beans from Mexico; Snap Beans from Karibean Island; Mayacoba Beans from Peru; Red Beans; Black Beans; White Beans; Vanilla Beans; and Ewa Oloyin Beans from Nigeria, too. He told them that the Beans are too plentiful and diverse to list them all. He referred them to the website for more insight on that topic.

Next, how will they get there? A debate ensued over two suggestions: fly in a swarm or hide out as stow aways on an airplane. After hearing all the reasons for and against each idea, a vote was taken. The majority wanted to go on the airplane because it would be a faster, safer free ride. Moreover, they would not have to make so many rest stops due to exhaustion from flapping their wings over thousands of miles.

Now, how can they make this happen? An elderly Locust suggested that they surreptitiously hide by attaching themselves to pieces of luggage before loading. Obviously they could not swarm in, but one by one or two by two, they could easily go unnoticed. This idea was met with unanimous approval.

Iru appointed Oku, an experienced traveler, to investigate and work out the logistics for the plane trip.

Regarding safety, they thought that they just needed to remain hidden and move individually or in pairs until they found a tree at or near the airport where they could gather to make further plans after landing in the U. S. Oku would remain in the airport to collect information on domestic flights that would take them to the Beanville District. When he had all the necessary information, he would fly out of the airport and reconnect with the group by using their language, Locustanese, which is foreign in the U. S. Absolutely no one would understand that Oku would be asking, "Where are you?" And Iru would reply, "We are over here." The tree would be their safety net until their next move toward Beanville.

Oku dived into gathering information and planning the trip. He found a flight for the first leg of the journey. It was a 14 hour, non-stop flight that would touch down in New York at JFK Airport at 9:00 AM on the second day of the reunion. Unfortunately, some international flights leave Nigeria only once a week. This one was their only option.

He thought that since they are tree Beans, they only need to find a tree to accommodate themselves until connections for a domestic flight could be found. They could eat and drink from the trees as well as from the ground.

A few days went by then it was time for the meeting. Those who had planned to go came to the "Meeting Tree." The only item on the agenda was preparations for the trip.

After Iru convened the meeting, he turned it over to Oku to outline his plans. Oku started by reviewing their last discussions and added that he had found the only flight for the trip. He gave them all the pertinent details related to airline, flight number, gate, date, and time. Having this information made them more ready for the trip. He ended with telling them that they would gather at the "Meeting Tree" three hours before flight time so that they could fly to the airport in small groups and hide themselves in the luggage before it gets loaded on the plane. Once they found a crevice to crawl into, they should speak in Locustanese that they were hidden so that Oku could account for everyone, 250 in all. Of course, Oku and those in his group would be the first to find their places.

After Oku's presentation, Iru was ready to answer questions, but there were none. Everyone felt ready to go. The meeting ended and they returned home.

When the day came for the big trip, plans were executed as detailed in the meetings. Being tree Beans, they did not have to hassle with things other travelers carry. They only needed to bring themselves.

Little by little they got to the airport, found hiding places, and waited patiently for take- off.

At last, the plane was loaded with luggage, passengers, the crew, and Locust Beans. It started moving on the runway. The lift off was smooth and incident free. Fourteen hours later, it landed at JFK in NY.

As the baggage was being unloaded and put on the conveyor, Locust Beans were coming out of crevices and searching for a nearby tree. Iru had positioned himself so that he would be among the first to get out in order to search for a large tree.

He did not have to look far. Near the baggage claim exit stood a huge gum tree. Iru signaled in Locustanese to join him in that tree.

Their spirits were high and they started celebrating their safe arrival in the USA. They were so thrilled that none of them could hold back their excitement.

So when Oku exited the airport and located the "Bean Tree," he told them that their next flight to Beanville District would be leaving in 2.5 hours. They needed to relocate to another side of the airport and begin hiding out as before. However, this time, under the cover of thick smog, they could swarm over and not be noticed.

Again, when the luggage, passengers, crew, and Locusts were loaded, the plane moved down the runway, lifted off, and this time headed toward the Beanville District landing 45 minutes later. It was a very short flight.

They followed the same procedure as before. Only this time, Oku exited the airport, too. Iru found the "Meeting Tree" and summoned the others over. They were fascinated to have arrived at their first destination in Beanville. Now, Oku had to survey and plan navigation to the water park, venue of the Bean Family Reunion.

Oku told Iru that he would fly around town and search for information that would lead them to the place. While waiting for Oku's return, Iru and the others relaxed in the branches of the tree and discussed their expectations for an exciting and memorable family reunion.

As Oku flew through the city, he noticed the roadside signage. He was specifically looking for signs leading to the Beanville Water Park.

After flying around for about fifteen minutes, he spotted the first sign for which he was in search. He followed the sign and ended up in the water park! Growing more and more excited, he explored the premises and the nearby community. He located the Beanville Luxury Inn & Suites and saw the marquee that read: "Bean Family-Welcome to Beanville." With all the information and directions that they needed, his level of enthusiasm heightened. Oku looked around a little longer. He spotted a group that appeared to be the Bean family. He flew closer in and listened to what was going on. Indeed, he had hit it. Bingo- the reunion! He was beside himself with joy and a sense of accomplishment. He flew back as fast as his wings could take him to the area where he had left the others.

Upon reaching the vicinity, he called out in Locustanese, "Tee-chi? Tee-chi? ("Where are you?") Iru replied, "Mi-ni. Mi-ni" ("Over here. Over here.")

Iru and the others were bursting with jubilation and anticipation of good news from Oku. Oku had to settle down for a few minutes before he could share his findings after having flown around for nearly one and a half hours in unfamiliar territory.

He relaxed for about ten minutes then called everyone to hear his report. He told them that they were not very far from the water park, about fifteen minutes away. He added that he had seen the fancy hotel that welcomed the Bean family. Also, he informed them that they would have absolutely no problems at the water park because there are many different kinds of trees scattered all over.

After hearing Oku's report, they calmed down and prepared themselves for their final destination at the water park. Oku mentioned that activities were under way, so they should immediately follow him to the water park and find a tree in a good spot where they could see and hear everything without obstructions.

Twenty minutes later, the Locust Beans were at the reunion, nestled in a tree and watching what was going on. Since they were late arrivals, they decided not to interrupt the activities with introducing themselves. They joined the reunion in silence without making their presence known for now. For them, it was still a treat and a rewarding experience to see the size and diversity of their family. The Vines and Bushes were spectacular, but it was even better seeing some other tree Beans similar to themselves.

They continued watching and listening until everyone disappeared and night fell upon the water park.

DAY 2 – SEPTEMBER 3
FUN AND GAMES

Night revolved into morning. At 7:00 AM, the family started arriving for breakfast. They knew what to expect and how to conduct themselves from the previous day. The music made breakfast an enjoyable time and foreshadowed what was coming upon the horizon for the day's activities. There was so much excitement in the air. They could hardly wait for breakfast to end.

From the Locusts' perspective, sitting high and looking low on everything was not bad at all. So for the rest of the day, that's what they did until the activities closed and everyone went their separate ways until the morning of the third and final day.

Time came for the games of the day to begin, so Jell stood up and said, "I hope you all had a good night, a good breakfast, and now you are ready for some fun. Are you ready?" she called. "Vine Beans, are you ready?" The vines responded, "Yes, we are." She asked the Bush Beans, "Are you ready?" There was a resounding reply, "We are more than ready!" Then Jell said, "Take your places – Vines left, Bushes right."

When they were in place, she told them that the first game was "Tug-of-War." She explained the rules and asked them to sub-divide into groups of ten. The oldest Beans chose to watch and be cheerleaders as the younger ones competed against each other.

They were all glad to see that the judges for the games were Jelly Beans who were neither vine nor bush Beans. Surely there would be no partiality in determining the winners.

Groups 1 of the Vines and Bushes tugged the bean pole as hard as they could. Just when it seemed as though the Vines were close to winning, the Bushes tugged a little harder and won round one.

A great roar along with whistling and clapping arose from the Bushes' side of the grounds. The Vines weren't silent. They cheered their team and proclaimed that round one was just a battle, not the war.

"Tug-of-War went on round after round until it was down to the final two teams. When the game ended, the Bushes emerged as winners. How excited they were. Jumping, clapping, and shouting resonated all over the park.

When the excitement quieted, the blue and red ribbons were awarded and the next game, "Bean Bag Basketfall" was ready. This time, the younger Beans were thrilled to reverse rolls and watch and cheer as the older Beans competed. Though there were not as many older Beans as there were younger ones, they had enough to form two teams with five players per team. Vines on the left and Bushes on the right.

The Bushes chose red bean bags while the Vines selected green ones. Everything was ready and so were the players.

Snappie was happy again because she was leading team 1, Vines, with the first throw. She threw her green bean bag and it went straight into the basket. Cheers went up for her as she danced to the back of the line. The next player on her team threw and made the basket, too. All of her other teammates made their baskets. Score: 5 – 0.

Team 1 for the Bushes started their throws. The first throw missed the basket. The second one missed. Throws three, four, and five fell into the basket yielding a score of 5:3 Vines.

Vines team 2 took their turn and ended with a score of 4. Bushes ended with a perfect score of 5. Thus the Bushes won this round.

To determine the winner of the game, the Vines' team 1 had to play the Bushes' team 2.

Round 3 had everyone's attention. Snappie and her team held hands and chanted, "We are Beans that grow on the vine, and we have the surest shot you're ever going to find." The Bushes retorted, "We are the best you've ever seen. Our shot is straight, mean, and clean." Jell let them keep it up for a few minutes. Then she said, "And now, it's time to see who the winner will be. Vines' team 1, take your places. Bushes" team 2 take your places." To determine who would throw first, they did a coin toss. Vines chose heads and Bushes had tails. Vines won the toss but decided to let the Bushes throw first.

The Bushes kept chanting, "We are the best you've ever seen. Our shot is straight, mean, and clean." The first player threw and the bag fell straight in the basket. Before throwing, the second player pulled a rabbit's foot out of his pocket, rubbed it, and returned it to its hiding place. He then took a very deep breath. With all eyes on him, he took a teeny weeny baby step then threw the bag. It landed on the rim for a brief second then fell into the basket. "Yeah! Right on! Way to go," the Bushes shouted.

Player number 3 took her place behind the line. She was nervous because of the commotions of chanting, cheering, whistling, and clapping. She called to them to be quiet and still so she could concentrate and focus on making a good shot. All the noise and movement came to a sudden stop. It was as quiet as cotton falling to the floor. She, too, stood completely frozen. Then she gracefully lifted her right hand holding the bag as if she were being filmed in slow motion and threw the bag straight into the basket. The silence and stillness burst into chanting, jumping, clapping, and various displays of excitement.

The successful throws of players 1,2, and 3 gave player 4 all the confidence he needed. He stepped up to the line, closed his eyes and took his shot. As quick as lightning, BAM! Another basket for the Bushes.

With no misses so far, the Bushes were exploding with happiness and positive vibes that they were going to get an uncontested score of 5. Just one more basket. They began to chant, "For a perfect score – All we need is just one more."

Player 5 stood behind the line. He knelt. He got up and twirled around. He took five steps backward and five steps forward. On his fifth step forward, he hurled the bag into the basket. Bingo! The Bushes had their chant ready. "We got it. We Got it. We got our perfect score. We got it. We got it. We don't need no more.!"

Now, what will the Vines do? Will they get a perfect score, too?

The Vines began to chant, "We'll match your score without any drama. Tell your daddy, sister, brother, and yo momma. After they repeated their chant a couple of times, Jell said, It's time to play. Vines Player number 1 step up to the line. Get ready. Begin."

As soon as Jell finished her announcement, player 1 threw. Bang! The bag landed in the basket. Player 2 threw. Whoosh! Basket hit. Player 3 – Basket. Player 4 – Pop! Basket. Player 5 – Boom - Basket. A perfect score in a flash.

The Vines began chanting again, "We matched your score without any drama. Go tell your daddy, sister, brother, and yo momma."

Incredible! Without any more drama, they had a 5 -5 tie. Of course, the tie had to be broken, which would be done after lunch.

They were so deeply buried in the fun and gleeful-ness that there were no thoughts about lunch until one hour past lunchtime.

During eating, as usual everything was quiet and still except music to set the tone of celebration, happi-ness, and fun. Though they ate in silence, they were anx-ious to see which team would win. They could hardly contain their anticipation of an exciting finish.

After ninety minutes, Jell made the announcement everyone had been waiting to hear.: "Lunch is over. Let's resume the game. Take your places. Vines on the left and Bushes on the right. Everyone else who was not on the playing teams scrambled to find a spot as close as possible to the teams for the tie breaking event.

When everyone was in place and the teams were ready, the chanting started with the Vines. "Bag in the basket on every throw whether we make it high or make it low." The Bushes countered, "We'll win this game with a score of five. That's a fact. It ain't no jive."

Again, a coin toss started the game. Vines won with heads. This time they elected to go first. Player 1, Happy Snappie, stepped up to the line. In the blink of an eye, she threw a high bag that looked like a fly ball. It zipped through the air and fell in the basket. An uproar of chanting erupted again: "Bag in the basket on every throw whether we make it high or make it low."

Snappie put on a show this time. She danced and chanted all the way to the end of her line feeling thrilled that she had not disappointed her team.

Player 2 stepped up, and without pausing, threw another bag that landed in the basket. Players 3, 4, and 5 wasted no time either and all made hits, straight in the basket. They had their score of five. The Vines broke out in their alarming chant, "Bag in the basket on every throw whether we make it high or make it low."

Since it was a competition, the Bushes aroused team spirit with their fight song, "We'll tie this game with a score of five. That's a fact. It ain't no jive."

Jell instructed the Bushes to take their first throw. They had made a pact that there would be no drama this time around. So each turn went quickly and smoothly from players 1-4. Zip! Zip! Zip! Zap! All falls in the basket. Player 5 was up. This time he stood in place and counted, "1,2,3,4." As he counted 5 he threw and sneezed simultaneously throwing off his aim at the basket. Though it momentarily landed on the rim, it ended on the ground.

'Oh, no! Oh, no! Oh, no!" He fell to his knees and cried. "How did this happen?" He realized that his team had lost the tie breaker 5 – 4. His team faced the agony of defeat, but did not beat him up too much. After all, they were family and it was just a game for fun.

On the other hand, the Vines realizing that they had won sang their chant with more gusto and vigor than ever. They expressed their elation with clapping, jumping, chest bumping, and hand pumping.

Jell declared the Vines' team 1 the winners and issued each of them a blue ribbon to bring closure to the activity. She congratulated them and offered consolation to the Bushes as she told them "Better luck next time." She issued their red ribbons indicating second place.

The day did not end there. One more game was scheduled for the youngest members of the family. It was Bean Bag Tic-Tat-Toe. They took a brief fifteen-minute intermission before the game got underway.

Since it was getting late, this game had to be a short one. Jell asked the teams to choose their players. When each team had chosen its players, they moved to the Tic-Tac-Toe board with bean bags in hand.

Inasmuch as the Vines had won the previous game, their player had the first "mark" on the board. Player 1 put his green bean bag in the center box. Bushes' player put her red bag in the upper center above the green bag. Green went in the upper right corner. Red in lower left corner. Green in lower right corner. Facing a two-way green win, red went in the upper left corner. Final play for the win, green went in the right center box.

Jell declared the Vines the winners. The thrill of victory could be heard not only all over the water park, but all the way to downtown city center a mile and a half away. It was the most exciting time for the Vines. They had won two of the three games: Bean Bag Basketfall and Tic-Tat-Toe while the Bushes had won only the Tug of War.

The Vines started singing songs about being champions and the music filled with invigoration and jubilee backed them up! Ribbons were awarded to the Tic-Tac-Toe participants and the group activities for the day ended, but not before Big Mama stood up and said how much fun she had had and was so glad that she had come. She thanked everyone for all the planning and work they had invested to make the event such a success. She told them that she was all fired up and already ready for the next reunion.

Pink and The GNB took turns thanking everyone for coming and expressed how elated they felt about the level of enthusiasm, attendance, and participation.

At the conclusion of all the speeches, Jell announced that everyone was free to explore the water park, the town, go shopping, or do whatever made them happy.

Before the final dismissal, she reminded them that tomorrow would be Day 3, the last day and breakfast would begin at the same time, same place, and same routines. However, it would only be a half day and that they would wrap up everything and close out this year's reunion with door prizes, recognitions, and a meeting to determine when and where the next Bean Family Reunion would be held.

After having said that, the family began departing going their own separate ways until the park looked deserted.

Being free to do as they pleased, that's just what they all did except the Soldier and Navy Beans who were keeping security in high gear throughout the evening and night. When one group had served its time, another group arrived and traded positions. The exchange of duties progressed unceremoniously unlike the Changing of the Guards in Washington D C, London, and other parts of the world.

SEPTEMBER 4 - DAY 3
THE DISASTROUS AMBUSH

Day 2 had been a day filled with fun, games of competition, chants, and performances. That day ended when everyone dispersed to various places and activities of choice.

The day turned into night and everyone went back to their living quarters and settled in for a restful and peaceful night while the Soldier and Navy Beans kept a night vigil over them at the hotels.

Night turned into day and it was getting close to breakfast time. Beans were showering, bathing, dressing, and packing to prepare themselves for the day and end of the reunion when most of them would be leaving Beanville. Expectations were at an all- time high. They would see grand-parents, aunts, uncles, and cousins once again. They would eat at the food stations and enjoy music. Door prizes would be awarded. They would learn a little about their family history, and vote on the venue of the next reunion. So much to do in so little time with only a half day today.

Breakfast started as the Beans began to arrive. At first there were just a few, but before long, every food station was occupied with old and young Beans alike. The music created a celebratory atmosphere.

After a while, Jell made an announcement that in ten minutes, the program for the day would begin.

In exactly ten minutes, she called the family to order. First on the agenda was giving away door prizes to keep up the interest and excitement.

Jell and her team had taped numbers to various places around the room. Prizes would go to the one nearest the number. Five Beans won prizes. Each one jumped for joy at winning.

The next item on the agenda was the family history given by The GNB. He stood and said that he could not be too historical because he did not know too much, but he would share the little nuggets that he did know. He began, "No one really knows exactly where, how, or when the Bean family started. However, we believe that we have been around since the creation of life in the Garden of Eden. Our genealogy wasn't recorded for so many generations. Nevertheless, here is the story of how Beans came to the USA. Garbanzo, nick-named Chickpea, met and married Pea in Mexico. Later they migrated to the USA, lived on a farm, and began to have offsprings. Their offsprings met and married many other kinds of Beans and Peas. Some remained in place and kept bearing more Beans and Peas while others got taken to so many countries around the world. It was almost like a Bean diaspora. When beans began traveling on their own, we became ubiquitous. No continent was Beanless. As you can see, here we are today with families from everywhere, every size, shape, and color.

I need to do a genealogical study of our family and have more to present to you at our next reunion. Thank you."

He had all ears through the duration of his brief speech. When he finished, they applauded and thanked him. Most of them commented that this was their first time hearing anything at all about the Bean family.

Pink stood and recaptured how the family union and reunion began. She, too, received applauses. Some had never heard her message either.

Meanwhile, the Locust Beans remained hidden safely in the tree listening to and observing all that was going on. Iru had planned to swarm down with all the others to introduce themselves and make their presence known.

Everything was rolling along so well and Jell was ready to entertain ideas about the next Reunion: When? Where? but very abruptly the Soldier and Navy Beans sounded alarms. "Run! Run! Run for your life!"

No one knew what was happening or how to respond. The Soldier and Navy Beans kept urging them to get out of the park as quickly as possible. "Leave everything! Run! Run! Pandemonium, shock, and chaos spread through the park as the Beans ran not knowing why they had to run or where they were running to.

As they ran, they saw human beings carrying nets, bean catchers, bags, sacks, and other unidentifiable objects in pursuit to capture them.

The water park and the town of Beanville were in an uproar! Beans and humans were on the run. The Beans were struggling to escape human captivity.

This ambush of the Beans had happened so suddenly! It was as if the humans had premeditated it for a long time because there were so many of them not only in the park, but at the hotels and all over the town.

Humans and Beans kept up this roundup for hours. Some Beans tried to hide but were found and taken captive. They had nowhere else to run and nowhere else to hide. Seemingly, there were more humans running than there were Beans. Eventually, the Beans had to surrender to the humans. Every human had captives – Beans of every size, shape, and color.

The Beans were left bewildered, dumbfounded, and helpless. It was unbelievable how such an ambush could have occurred so swiftly disrupting and disorganizing their family reunion. What started out as a beautiful, well-planned day quickly transformed into a gloomy, dreadful, and fearful one. It was the most horrific day in the life of every Bean. More terrifying than any of them could have imagined! With most of them captured and scattered all over everywhere, what could they do next?

Those few who managed to escape found a way to disguise themselves well enough to sneak past the human stakeouts and checkpoints. They exited Beanville

by any means they could. Taxis, buses, trains, and subways met their urgent need to get away.

Where did they go? They went to a neighboring farm town called Greenville where they managed to hideout for a few days in the fields with the crops that were springing up and sprouting.

They were not able to organize themselves and work together to evade capture. It was every man for himself. No one knows exactly where they went after leaving Greenville. The only certainty is that they got out and never returned.

As for the captives, theirs is a different story. The humans did so many things with them that we still do today.

It was so pitiful to see how such an ambush could terrorize the Bean family and terminate their family reunion forever.

EXIT OF THE LOCUST BEANS

Watching what was happening to their family, they cried out in horror stricken voices, but they got no attention or response. What could they do about this calamity? They could not frighten the humans away by swarming down because pest control might have been called out to exterminate them. They thought about a number of actions, but their safety would be jeopardized. So they decided to stay in the tree and helplessly succumb to the demise of their family.

Had they tried to intervene and gotten exterminated, the family back home in Nigeria would forever wonder about what happened and why none of them returned to tell the story of their venture. Therefore, Iru and Oku convinced the others that for their safety, it was best for them to shelter in place until the disturbance had completely died out then they could steal away as quietly and as unnoticed as they had come.

Oku, however, had to get to the airport and find their departing flight so that they could leave as soon as possible. With a heavy heart and deep sympathy, he flew out and gathered information. He found a flight scheduled for 12:00 AM the following day with connections at JFK in NY for Lagos, Nigeria.

He returned to his grief ridden family and imparted to them the details of the flight then settled down and grieved with them while waiting for the hour of their departure. It was a very sorrowful and painful wait as time drifted by.

At last it was time to leave the tree and head to the airport. They repeated their previous routines and ended up at their point of origin.

Once they arrived in Lagos, they found a domestic flight which took them back to their township with the story of the awful outcome of the Bean Family Reunion.

When they met at the "Meeting Tree," they, as survivors, told their eyewitness encounters leaving everyone to speculate that there would never be another attempt to have another Bean Family Reunion.

Indeed, they waited for years for news of a family reunion, but none ever came. Those who went carried visions and flashbacks with them for the remainder of their lives. They shared the story with their children and their children's children.

CHAPTER 8

What the Beans Did Not Know

The biggest story in the history of Beanville came across the TV and radio stations as breaking news. All of the news media from Beanville and surrounding towns found their way to the water park, hotels, the subway station, and other nearby businesses to be there to start coverage as soon as the ambush began.

They had all been tipped off about the ambush of the Beans and asked to operate on a code of secrecy and silence so that the Beans would be under attack without the slightest expectation.

While the Beans were enjoying the last day of their family reunion, news media was preparing to capture their ambush. There were cars, trucks, and vans all over the water park. Gazette, Times Herald, Tribune, was pasted to the sides of some vehicles while WBQN, WAFD, WRON, or WUPP were on others.

When everything was in place and reporters with camera crews were waiting in presupposition for a major catastrophe, they heard a human voice over a megaphone say, "Let's do it!" They aggressively charged the security guards. It was too late for the Soldier and Navy Beans who were under attack first. Most of them became human captives as others ran toward the area where the Beans were meeting. They were screaming, "Run! Run! Run for your life."

Every television and radio station was airing this news live on the scene as it was happening. There appeared to be more boots than roots on the ground. Beans on roots and humans on foot. Beans were running as fast as their roots could carry them, but not fast enough to avoid becoming hostages to the humans who came prepared with equipment and gadgets to catch them.

What the Beans did not know is that a professor of nutrition, Prof. Ryce Peabody, at the University of Beanville had been conducting a very extensive and confidential study on beans and with approval of his dean, he was gradually and secretly releasing his findings to citizens of Beanville, surrounding areas, and throughout the country.

The professor had found that beans are a consumable plant protein that had a long history of being eaten by animals and humans alike. Beans have been eaten in so many ways. For example, beans have been boiled or refried then eaten alone or added to other dishes to enhance the flavor. They have been used to make delicious soups, dips, salads, stews, and side dishes.

Because he was ambitious and wanted to make a name for himself, perhaps the "Bean Wizard of the World," he published an overview of his research in a well-known nutritional journal, "For Human Consumption," and interviewed on a few television talk shows.

He was aware through "Bean Book," "Beanstagram," and "Beanknitter," that the Beans were having a three-day family reunion. Though he was not a part of the Bean family, he had an account with their social media networks to keep abreast of their activities.

He devised a "Grapevine News Network (GNN) to covertly invite other humans to come join him in getting as many free beans as they wanted to take home and do their own experimentations. After all, he concluded, "In the ecosystem, beans are producers. They are NOT humans as they are pretending to be."

"Was it some kind of magic bean that had cast a spell on the Beans to personify them?" He continued, "Beans acting like people is pure fantasy. If they are under a spell, it will be broken when we catch them, cook them, can them, bag them, box them, sack them, freeze them, and eat them. Tree Beans will be ground and used to make beverages.

Since beans are producers and there are so many kinds, sizes, shapes, and colors, beans will never wind up being in jeopardy of becoming extinct and people all over the world can enjoy them now and forever."

Professor Peabody had credibility after having worked at the university for over 20 years and published articles in renown magazines and journals as well as made appearances on TV. Using his GNN, he had planned a successful underground attack on the Beans. Humans came from all over to get their share of beans to tryout what Prof. Peabody had proclaimed about them. The humans were just as diverse as the Beans. Among the bean catchers could be found all ages, sizes, shapes, and colors.

Each of the humans did as the professor had admonished. They took their beans home, experimented with them, and met no disappointment.

CHAPTER NINE

Silence of the Beans

No more walking, talking Beans! Professor Peabody's released research shut down the personification of the Beans, therefore, no more human beans!

Humans were led to discover once again that beans are plants, green producers in the ecosystem. Humans also learned that bean DND is quite different from human DNA.

Once the professor had irrefutably established that beans can never be humans or any other animal, he worked fervently to erase ideas that the capture of the beans was inhumane and cruel.

A local TV station hired him as a part-time reporter for a program called, "Humans vs Beans." After approximately 20 shows, he felt confident that he had dispelled all myths and misconceptions about beans and that humans could feel free to do with beans whatever they wanted without any feelings of cannibalism or mistreatment. After all, beans are part of the plant kingdom.

Prof. Peabody had carefully outlined the content of his shows. First and foremost, he proved that beans cannot talk or make any sounds. They did not even have a mouth. They drink and ingest through their roots which are anchored in soil or water.

In his next show, he displayed several types of beans. Some he cut. There was no blood and no ouch - silence. He threw some of the beans into a pot of boiling water, 212 degrees Fahrenheit. There was no screaming. When the beans got soft, he eventually mashed them without even a murmur. "Here," he said. "It is clear to see that beans have no voice and no feelings."

In another show, he demonstrated that beans cannot walk or run independently moving from one place to another. As he had shown in a previous segment, their roots are planted in the soil. They move when the wind blows or some other organism or water transports them to other places. He joked and showed that jumping beans and magic beans are exceptions to bean movement.

At the conclusion of Professor Peabody's reports, the major TV stations added to their lineup, cooking and art segments demonstrating how to cook and use beans in creative ways.

After having so masterfully making it known to the public that beans are plants good for human consumption, Prof. Peabody went back to his full-time research at the university with intentions of targeting a different plant to research.

Humans were positively convinced beyond any and all doubt that they could indeed handle beans in a variety of ways such as cook, eat, and make creative things. They could even use them to teach kids basic mathematical skills like counting, adding, subtracting, multiplying, and dividing.

No matter what is done to any bean anywhere regardless of its kind, size, shape, or color, one thing is

indisputable, there will be no display of emotion or movement. Most notably, there will be no sound – silence.

With Prof. Peabody's research being totally accepted, people all over the world started eating and enjoying beans again at home. Restaurants as well resumed cooking and serving beans in a variety of ways.

Beans are back on the menu to stay and never to be removed again at any foreseeable time in the future.

CHAPTER TEN

Meet the Beans and Peas

BEANS FROM A – Z

Adzuki Bean

Anasazi Bean

Arabica Bean

Big Mama Bean

Black Bean

Black Eye Bean

Black Turtle Bean

Borlotti Bean

Broad Bean

Butter Bean

Calypso Bean

Cannellini Bean

Castor Bean

Cherokee Trail of Tears Bean

Cocoa Bean

Coffee Bean

Cowpea

Cranberry Bean

Dot Eye Bean

Dragon Tongue Bean

Dutch Bullet Bean

Ewa Oloyin (Honey) Bean

Eye of the Goat Bean (Ojo de Cabra)

Fava Bean

Flageolet Bean

Garbanzo Bean (Ceci/ Chickpea)

Good Mother Stallard Bean

Great Northern Bean

Green Bean

Haricot Bean

Ireland Creek Annie Bean

Jack Bean

Jacob's Cattle Bean (Trout/Dalmation Bean)

Jelly Bean

Kentucky Wonder Bean

Kenyan Bean

Kidney Bean

Lab-Lab Bean (Hyacinth)

Liberian Bean

Lima Bean

Locust Beans (Carob)

Lupini Bean

Magic Bean

Marfax Bean

Mayacoba Bean

Milk Bean

Molasses Face Bean

Mung Bean

Navy Bean

Orca Bean (Yin Yang Bean)

Pea Bean

Pink Bean

Pinto Bean

Polyanthus Bean

Preacher Bean

Provider Bean

Purple King Bean

Purple Queen Bean

Rattlesnake Bean

Red Bean

Red Swan Bean

Roman Bean

Royal Burgandy Bean

Runner Bean

Snap Bean

Soldier Bean

Soy Bean

Split Pea

String Bean

Sword Bean (Gladiata Bean)

Tiger's Eye Bean

Tongue of Fire Bean

Turkey Craw Bean

Urad Bean

Vanilla Bean

Wax Bean

White Bean

White Rice Bean

Winged Bean

Yard Bean (Asparagus Bean, Long bean)

Yellow Eye Bean

Zolfino Bean

This story about the Bean Family Reunion is a fantasy, not a fact.

However, the ubiquitous bean is real. Take the bean challenge!

Find more beans.

AUTHOR'S BIOGRAPHY

Anna M. Ridley Etuk is a retired educator who taught for over forty years in the state of Texas and the country of Nigeria in West Africa.

She is a native of Baton Rouge, Louisiana where she grew up in a family that maintained the tradition of having a family reunion for as long as she can remember up to the present. The fun, food, and fellowship with the old as well as the young and those who come from far and near always make the reunion a memorable family affair.

Usually, one of the special dishes at the reunion is red beans, rice, and cornbread. Most times, relatives from New Orleans prepare the beans with various types of meat from sausage to fried pig tails.

Memories of the beans at the reunion inspired investigation of beans and the writing of this book.